The Lost Ornament

Written by: Max Barnaby

Illustrated by: Tessa De Voe

For Mommy

December was here and excitement was brewing throughout the attic.
All year long the Christmas decorations waited for this time of year.
Finally, they would be taken out of their dusty boxes, and they would be brought downstairs.
The decorations knew that they only had this month to bring joy to the world, so they were eager to shine!

The attic was packed with boxes filled with every Christmas decorations you could imagine. There was garlands, candles, wreaths, nutcrackers, bows, linens, and so much more.
Regardless of how many decorations there were, each decoration was needed to create the magic of Christmas.

That cold December morning, the usually quiet attic was full of activity. The first decorations to go down were the lights, and they were ready to

Brighten

the house inside and out.

Next, the stockings went down.   They were ready
to add more warmth to the toasty fireplace.

Then went the inflatable snowman, which was followed by
the "Merry Christmas" welcome mat

After 11 months of constantly reenacting Luke 2, the nativity was ready to be carefully brought down into their place of honor on the fireplace mantle.

Last but not least, the tree skirt and the ornaments were taken out of the attic. Oh the ornaments! So many ornaments! Many memories were stored in each ornament, and what joy they brought when they were hung on the tree.
Christmas was coming to life throughout the home.

After a long hard day of Christmas decorating, the attic was finally empty of all Christmas decorations. Or was it?
In a dark corner, there sat a small dusty box that no one seemed to notice.

That box held a very little ornament. There was nothing really special about this ornament.
It was just an old wooden carved lamb with the white paint chipping off of it.

Once the quiet returned to the attic, the lamb peered out of the box.
She looked around and didn't see any of her friends.

Gone were the chatty bells, gone were the shiny tinsels, and gone was the lively Christmas gnomes with their tippy red hats. Where was everyone? The little lamb began to wonder,

"Am I the only Christmas decoration left behind?"
She tried to wait patiently,
"Maybe they would notice I'm missing, and soon I'll be down hanging on the soft evergreen tree with all the other ornaments. "

The days rolled by... December 4th, 8th, 16th... the little lamb was still in that corner.

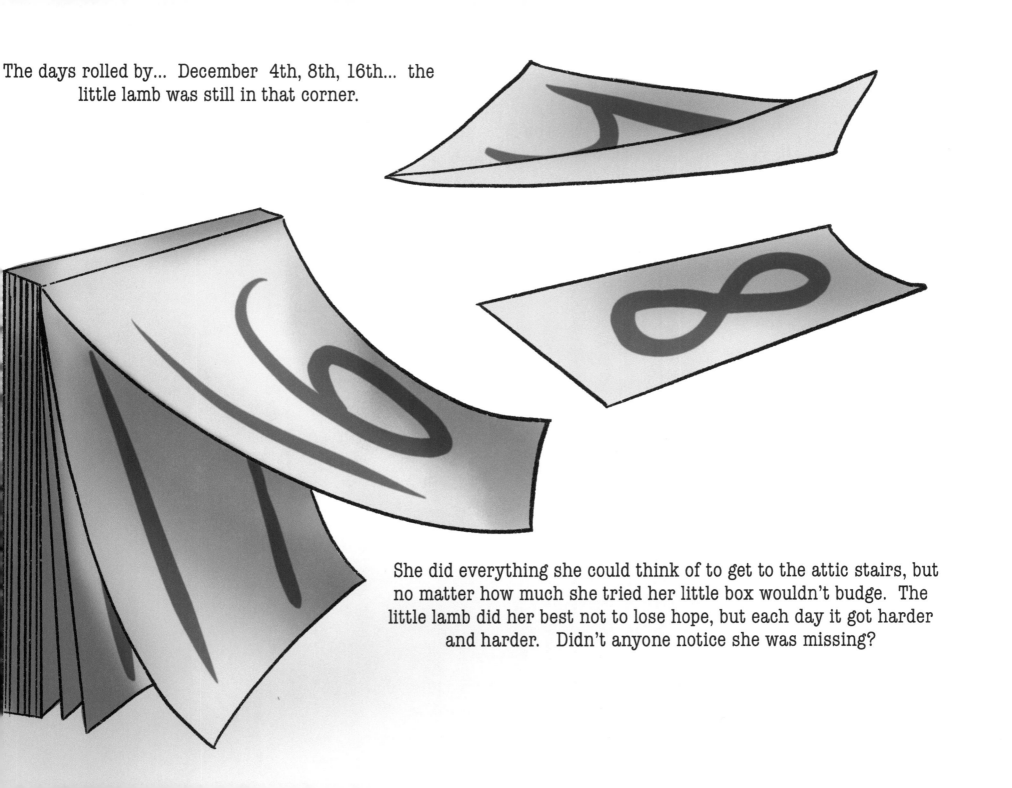

She did everything she could think of to get to the attic stairs, but no matter how much she tried her little box wouldn't budge. The little lamb did her best not to lose hope, but each day it got harder and harder. Didn't anyone notice she was missing?

As December 24th came, the little lamb realized the tree would be decorated by now.
"No one noticed I was missing. I guess I'm not needed,"
said the discouraged little lamb.
Perhaps she would forever sit in the attic, collecting dust and losing more paint.

Tears began to well up in the little lamb's eyes as she gave up her last bit of hope.
Suddenly, she was startled out of her sadness by loud, fast footsteps coming up the stairs.
"Who could that be so late on Christmas Eve?" thought the lamb.

She heard rummaging and muttering , as boxes were moved around quickly.
After what seemed like a long time, the box that held the little sheep began
to move.

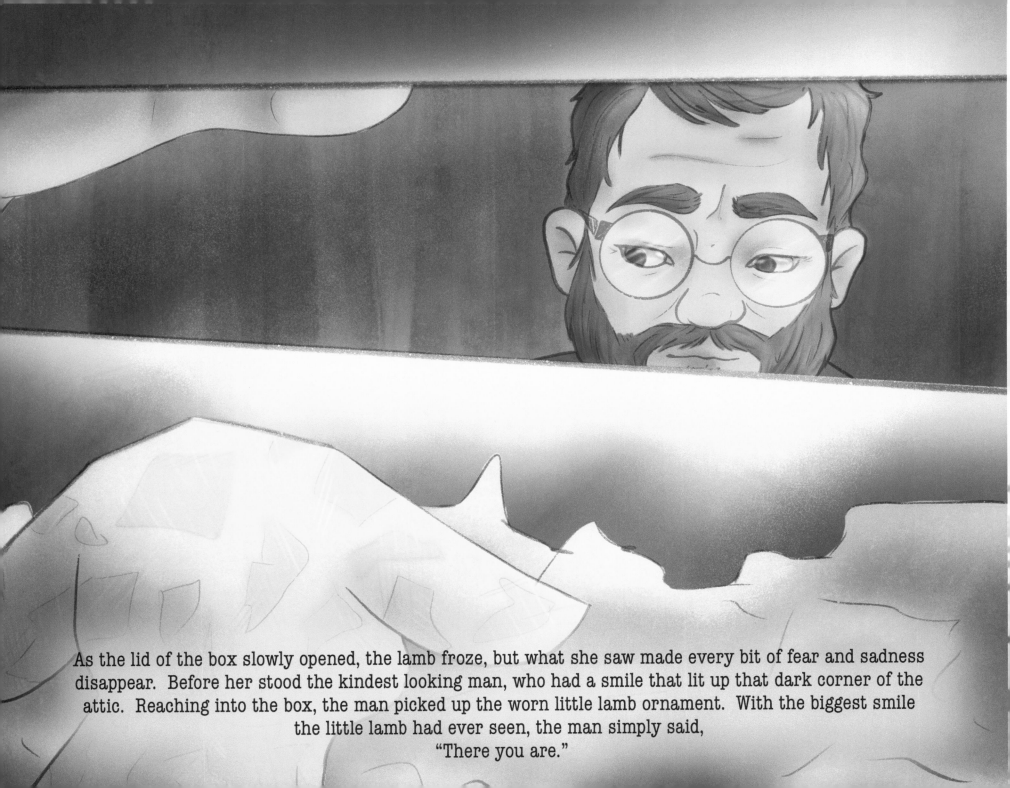

As the lid of the box slowly opened, the lamb froze, but what she saw made every bit of fear and sadness disappear. Before her stood the kindest looking man, who had a smile that lit up that dark corner of the attic. Reaching into the box, the man picked up the worn little lamb ornament. With the biggest smile the little lamb had ever seen, the man simply said,

"There you are."

Luke15:4-5

What man of you, having an hundred sheep, if he lose one of them, doth not leave the ninety and nine in the wilderness, and go after that which is lost, until he find it? And when he hath found it, he layeth it on his shoulders, rejoicing.

CPSIA information can be obtained
at www.ICGtesting.com
Printed in the USA
BVHW051945291120
593919BV00001B/6